AF633343

Young Learner's

My First Book of ACTION WORDS

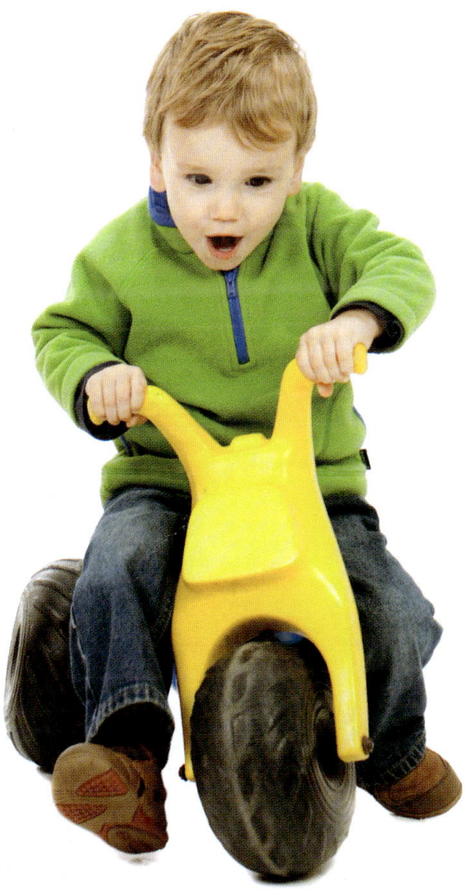

© Young Learner Publications®, India

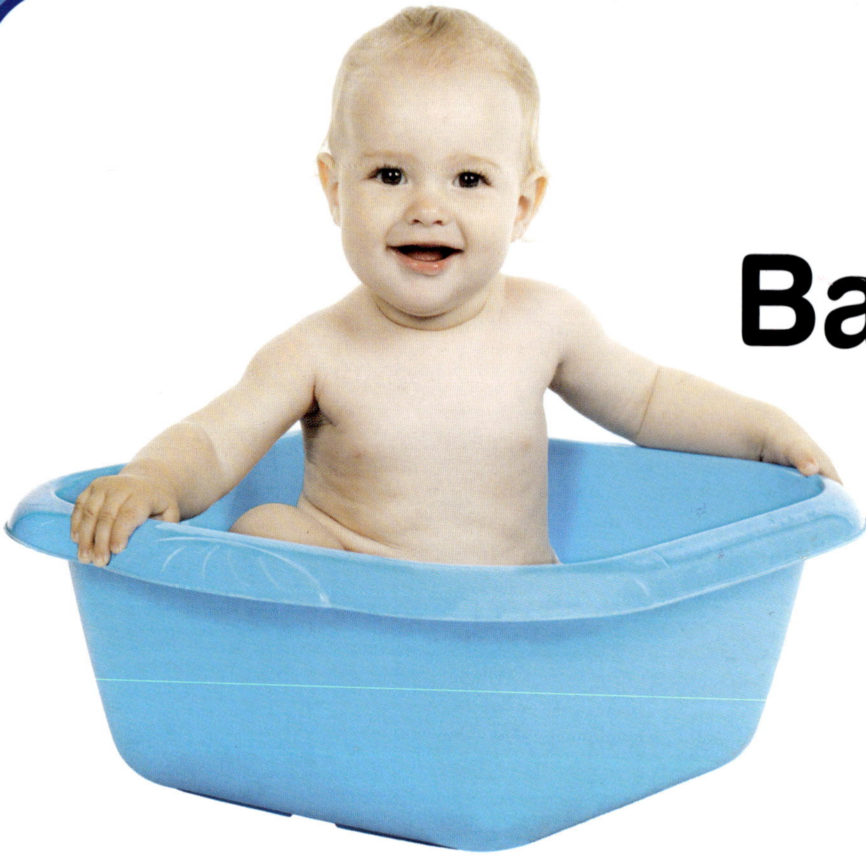

Bathing

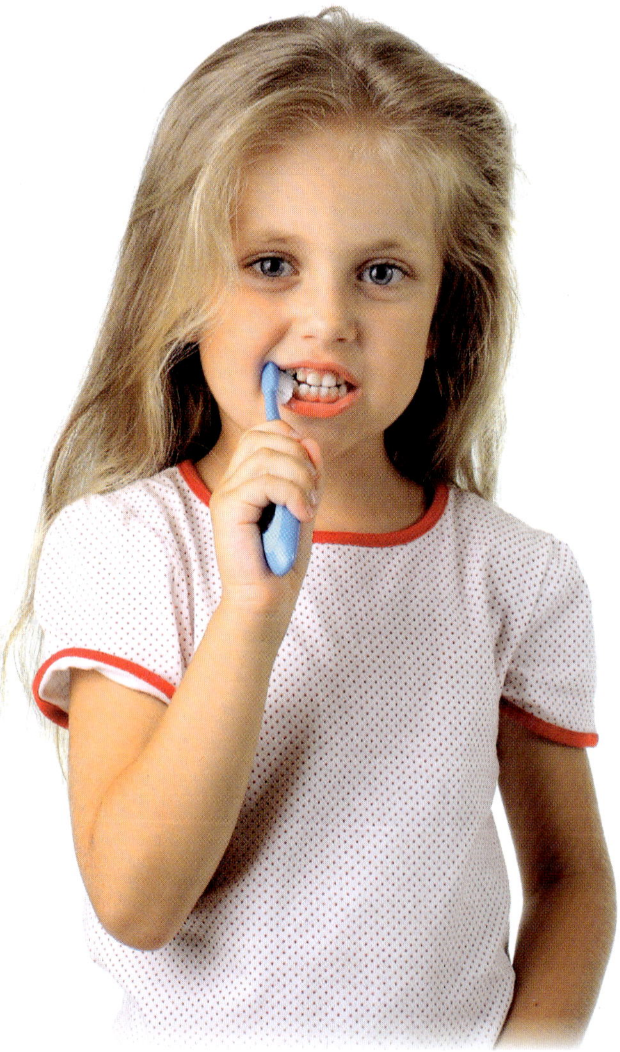

Brushing

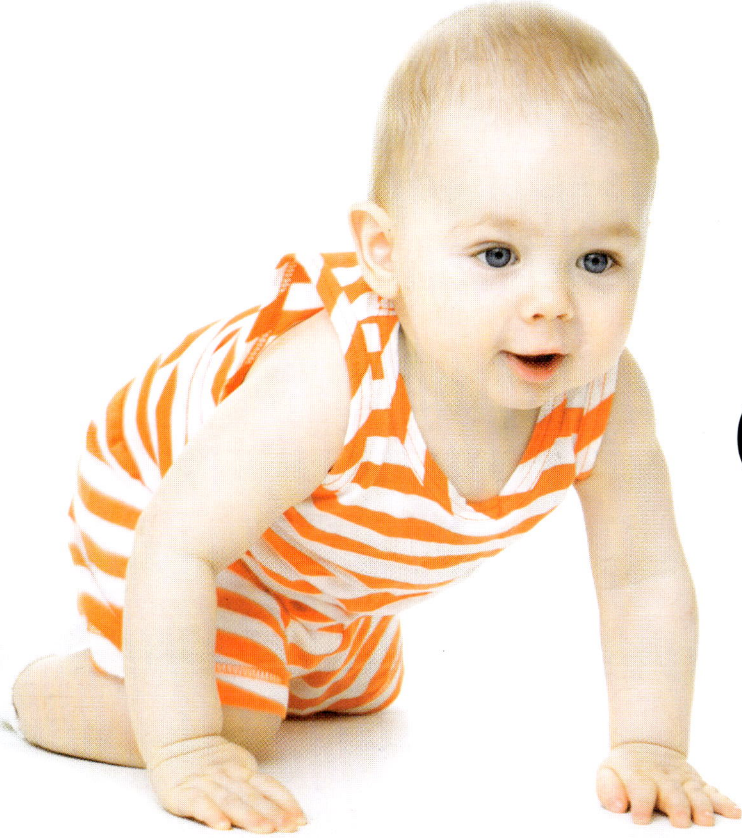

Crawling

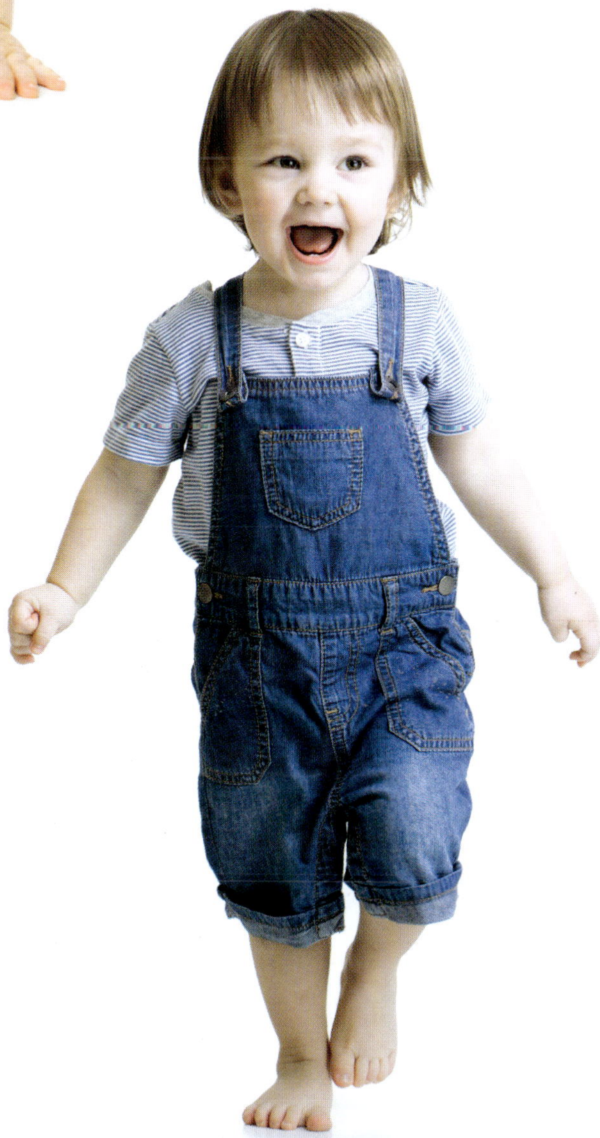

Walking

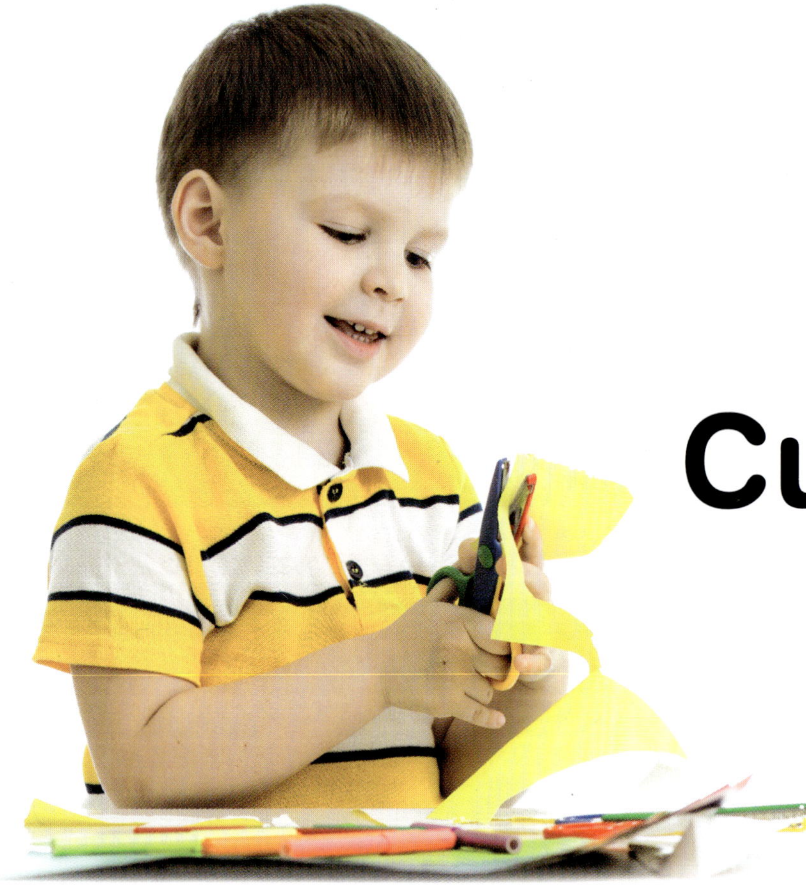

Cutting

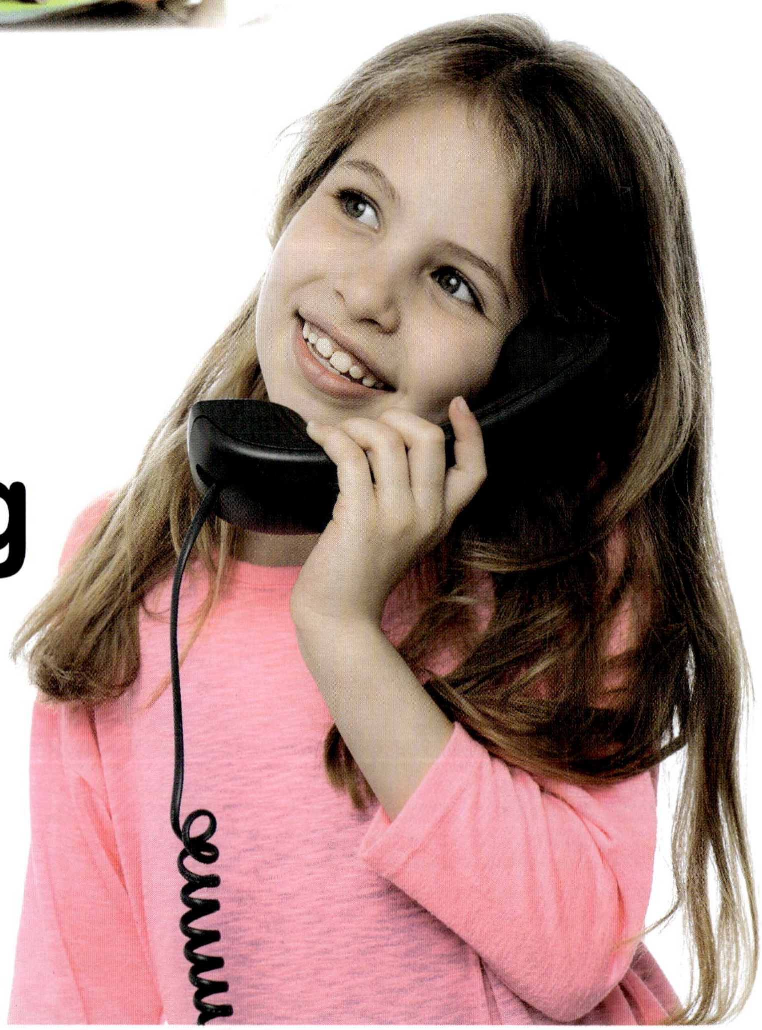

Talking